When Joel Comes Home

SUSI GREGG FOWLER

Pictures by **JIM FOWLER**

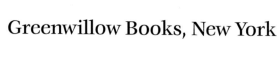

Greenwillow Books, New York

Watercolor paints and colored pencils
were used for the full-color art.
The text type is ITC Veljovic Medium.
Text copyright © 1993 by Susi Gregg Fowler
Illustrations copyright © 1993 by Jim Fowler

Printed in Hong Kong by
South China Printing Company (1988) Ltd.
First Edition   10 9 8 7 6 5 4 3 2 1

Library of Congress Cataloging-in-Publication Data

Fowler, Susi L.
When Joel comes home / by Susi Gregg Fowler ;
illustrated by Jim Fowler.
p.   cm.
Summary: A little girl describes all the things
she and her parents are planning to welcome home
friends and their newly adopted son.
ISBN 0-688-11064-9 (TR).   ISBN 0-688-11065-7 (LE)
[1. Adoption — Fiction. 2. Friendship — Fiction.]
I. Fowler, Jim, ill.   II. Title.
PZ7.F82975Wh   1993
[E] — dc20   92-7979   CIP   AC

For my grandmother Inez Gregg
—S.G.F.

For my mother, Helen Fowler Surrell
—J.F.

"When Joel comes home," I said, "I will wear my best dress and my patent leather shoes. People at the airport will think I am going to a party, but a new baby is better than a party."

"When Joel comes home," I said, "we'll get up before sun-
rise because the plane comes in so early. But I won't
have any trouble waking up, I'll be so excited. When Joel
comes home, we'll probably sing all the way to the airport, we'll be so happy."

"When Joel comes home," I said, "we'll unroll the WELCOME HOME sign with Mom's fancy writing and my pictures."

I hoped the pictures would look right. We'd never seen Joel, since Jean and George had just adopted him. They're my parents' best friends, so I knew how to draw them, but I was just guessing about Joel. Mom said not to worry, they'd figure it out.

"When Joel comes home," I said, "I'll pick the most beautiful flowers from our garden. When Jean walks off the plane, I will give them to her and say, 'These are for you, because now you're a mom just like my mom.'"
Mom said Jean would like that.

"But best of all," I said, "when Joel comes home, I get to
hold him before anyone else. George promised. I can
hardly wait!"
"Jean and George had to wait a long time for Joel," Mom
said. "Surely we can stand to wait just a little while."

It seemed to me as if we'd waited forever. Finally the waiting was almost over. George and Jean were coming home with Joel the next morning.

I went to bed early, but it was hard to get to sleep. I kept trying to imagine what Joel would be like. Then it was hard getting up so early! I couldn't stop yawning.

I tried to dress in a hurry, but two of the buttons on my party dress popped off, so I had to wear my jumpsuit instead. Then I couldn't find one of my patent leather shoes. But it was raining, anyway, so I decided to just wear my boots.

"Hurry up and get in the car," Daddy said.
I think he was having trouble waking up, too.

"But I have to pick the flowers for Jean."
"Speed it up, then," he said. "We're running late."
The flowers were a little droopy, but I figured they'd
be better when they dried off.

Then Mom slammed the door on our sign. It ripped!
"Oh, honey, I'm so sorry," she said.
But we didn't have time to fix it.

Mom and Daddy drank coffee in the car, and I curled up
against the door and almost fell asleep again. Maybe we
would sing on our way home.

When we got to the airport, no one asked if I was going
to a party. I didn't look very fancy, after all, but I didn't
care anymore. I was thinking about Joel.
"Look, there's Zoe," I said, "and Christopher and Sam and
Ruby and Ryan and—practically everybody we know!"

Balloons on strings, bouquets of flowers, cameras, and smiles filled the arrivals lounge, even though it was still early morning.

"It's like a party!" I said.

"Announcing the arrival of Flight 67," said the voice on
  the loudspeaker.
  We ran to the window and watched Joel's plane touch
  down. Then we waited and waited while other people
  came up the ramp.
"Joel sure does make us wait!" I said.

"There they are," cried Mom.
Everything started happening at once. We pulled out our sign, and Daddy ran forward and started taking pictures. People began cheering and clapping.
Jean and George just laughed out loud when they saw all their friends. And Joel looked startled!

I ran up to give Jean my flowers.
She hugged me, and then she hugged Mom, and the next
thing I knew, everyone was hugging and laughing and
crying. You couldn't move without bumping into
someone—but nobody cared. We were all too happy.

"My arms are getting a little tired," I heard George say.
"I'll take him. I'll hold him," lots of people offered, but
  George was looking for me.

I sat down in one of the airport chairs and held out my arms. George sat down next to me and very gently placed Joel right in my lap.

Joel looked at me and wrinkled up his nose.
"Hey, Joel," I said. "I've been waiting for you!"
"We were all waiting for each other," said George.
I said, "Well, I'm glad the waiting is over. Now the
fun can begin!"